AND SO CAN SHE

Written by Lauren Bresner　　Illustrated by Carolyn Parks

And So Can She
Published by EduMatch®

PO Box 150324, Alexandria, VA 22315

www.edumatch.org

© 2022 Lauren Bresner, Carolyn Parks

All rights reserved. No portion of this book may be reproduced in any form without permission from the publisher, except as permitted by U.S. copyright law. For permissions contact:

sarah@edumatch.org

ISBN: 978-1-953852-59-5

There was a young girl,
big dreams filled her mind.

She sat with her mother
Who taught her to see

That **girls** impact the world

Not just those who are *he*.

Her mother said...

He may navigate the skies...

Or sail the deep blue sea.

Well, yes, little one.
And so can *she*.

He may fight fierce fires...

Or save a cat from a tree.

Well, yes, little one.
And so can *she*.

He may hit a homerun...

Or slam dunk on TV.

Well, yes, little one.
And so can *she*.

He may defend someone on trial
Or keep order in the court...

SMACK! 1, 2, 3!

He may coach college football

Or teach first grade PE...

Well, yes, little one.

And so can **she.**

He may run for president...

Or fight to keep the country free.

Well, yes, little one.
And so can *she*.

He may graduate from college
Or hold a Ph.D...

Then mother whispered to her daughter one final notion.

"Come, listen closely," she said with devotion.

He may one day change the world
And yet so may *she*.

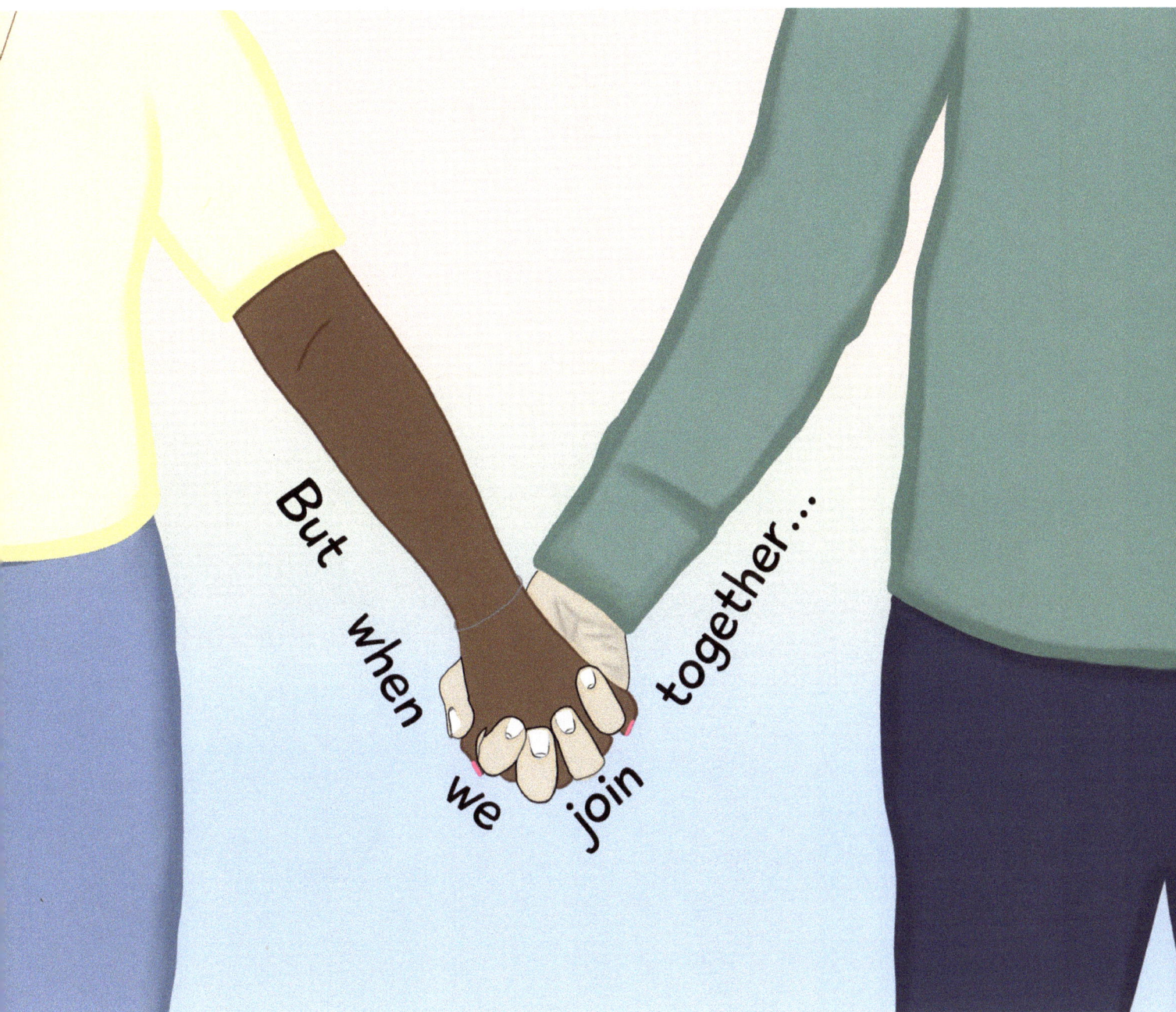

So can WE.

About the Author

Lauren Bresner is a special educator and mother. She grew up in New Jersey and now resides in Western Massachusetts with her husband, Alex, a college football coach, and daughter, Lucy, who inspired this story.

As a "girl mom" and female herself, Lauren is ambitious about creating a better world for women. Through her writing, she uses her passion for gender equality and expertise in elementary education to empower children to pursue their dreams, never letting gender restrict their choices.

CPSIA information can be obtained
at www.ICGtesting.com
Printed in the USA
BVHW021548110122
625990BV00015B/1048